THE REINDEER AFRAID TO FLY

Rusty was one of Santa's very special reindeer. He loved prancing in the snow at the North Pole, watching the elves make toys in Santa's workshop, and playing reindeer games.

But there was one thing Rusty didn't like. He didn't like to fly.
And flying was a very important part of being one of Santa's
reindeer. Every Christmas Eve, the reindeer carried Santa and
his sleigh all around the world to deliver toys. And this was the
year that Rusty was supposed to join the team.

"You're old enough now to help pull Santa's sleigh," Rusty's dad said, "it's a big honor. I remember the first time I flew with the team. I was a little afraid, but after the first few stops, I was fine."

Rusty still did not want to pull Santa's sleigh. He wanted to stay on the nice, safe ground and prance in the snow.

Rusty's friend, Speedy, had an idea. "I'll help you practice and then you can fly with us on Christmas Eve," Speedy said. Rusty was still unsure, but he agreed to try.

The next day, Speedy took Rusty out for his first flying lesson.
"Ready for takeoff?" Speedy asked. "Not really," Rusty replied.
"Come on," Speedy said, "you can do it. I know you can."
Rusty made a running start and then came to a stop. "I can't do it!"
exclaimed Rusty, hanging his head.

"Yes, you can," Speedy replied, trying to encourage his friend. "Watch me!" Speedy sprang into the air, flew in a circle and then gently landed. "See? Now it's your turn!" exclaimed Speedy.

"You make it look so easy," Rusty said.
"I bet you were never afraid to fly."

"Sure I was," Speedy replied. "Every reindeer is afraid at first, but the more you practice, the better you get, and the more fun it is to fly," Rusty wasn't convinced.

"I've got it!" shouted Speedy. He had an elf hook up a harness that connected the two reindeer. "I'll take off into the air and then pull you along," explained Speedy, "that way we'll be flying together." Speedy began to run with Rusty right behind him. With a big leap Speedy was in the air and so was Rusty!

"Now, close your eyes Rusty," Speedy said, "trust me." Rusty reluctantly closed his eyes as Speedy untied the harness. "Open your eyes," instructed Speedy. Rusty opened his eyes and saw an amazing sight. "I'm flying!" Rusty exclaimed. "I'm flying all by myself!"

It was Christmas Eve and time to deliver the presents to boys and girls all over the world. Santa assembled his reindeer.

"A special reindeer is joining us this year for his first trip," Santa announced, as he decorated Rusty's antlers, "a very special reindeer that is no longer afraid to fly."